Christmas Stories From Enoch

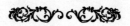

CHRISTMAS STORIES
FROM ENOCH
by
Douglas Newton

CHRISTMAS STORIES FROM ENOCH
©1988 by Douglas Newton

Published by Mary's Place Publishing,
a division of Mary's Place, Inc.
571 Stump Bluff Road
Bowling Green, KY 42101

Visit our Web site at www.marysplace.org

Printed in the United States of America.
First Printing: December 1988
Second Printing: January 2005

ISBN 0-9748257-0-0

To Margie, whose tender love
has freed me to imagine, create,
and know that God is good.

Table of Contents

Preface

If it is the case, as the Bible teaches, that we mortals may sometimes "entertain angels unaware," that angels can actually walk this earth, and talk our language, and sit in our homes, and share our meals, might it not be possible that on occasion a mortal could do the same in the world of the angels?

All I needed was the smallest hint of a nod from scripture to go ahead and imagine what a human being, full of curiosity, might discover among the angels and then return to earth to share with his people. The approving nod came through one simple, yet rather mysterious, verse which speaks of a character named Enoch. Hebrews 11:5. One day he suddenly could not be found, so it says. The explanation offered? He was taken by God from the earth without experiencing death.

Once I went so far as to imagine him involved in heavenly affairs, it was not much of a leap of faith to imagine him also returning to earth on divine assignments. What resulted were simple stories of criss-crossing kingdoms, where angels and humans could share discoveries and assignments.

This cosmology became a vehicle for relaying my one deep, abiding faith. God is good. Nothing good on earth happens apart from Him. Since Christmastime is so full of good traditions, it's hard to imagine anything less than His intentional involvement in the origin of those traditions.

And so, between 1980 and 1987, Enoch has "come" to me once a year to tell me one new story about the origin of some Christmas traditions.

Of course, the stories are not literally true. And you will need to make that clear to young children. But don't let the stories become purely fictional, either.

The stories are not meant to be read in order, necessarily. They were not written, nor printed, in chronological order. Indeed, if God is timeless, then believing God to be restricted to a chronological order of events would be as anthropomorphic as believing He has hands and feet.

These stories were first written to be read aloud annually to my church congregation. To be animated by a storyteller's voice, face, and body. Please try reading them aloud—even if you're reading them privately. Tell yourself the story, don't just read it silently. Better yet, practice, and then read one aloud in the living room with your family at Christmastime.

Doug Newton

Christmas 1988

Introduction

My name is Enoch. No last name, just Enoch. I was born before a person needed a last name. During my lifetime on earth several thousand years ago, I tried my best to do whatever God wanted me to do.

One day I was walking and talking with God, and— believe it or not—He transported me to heaven in an instant. I didn't die. I just went straight to heaven. He said He was proud of my tendency to obey Him and that He could use a human of my type in some special assignments.

So for the past few thousand years, I have been involved in many of the most fascinating and important heavenly affairs of all time. Some of my assignments had to do with what you know as Christmas, the first one when Jesus was born, and many more since. I've been used in heaven and on earth in some very important ways, and I've learned a lot of "behind the scenes" information that scratches my curiosity itch.

Recently, my assignment has been to come to earth at Christmastime and relay this information through one new story each year.

My only regret is that you didn't experience these wonderful heavenly events first-hand. But, then again, your day is coming… So, for now, the stories will have to do.

HOW THE CHRISTMAS TREE CAME TO BE

My name is Enoch, I am a human being who has had the rare opportunity to walk right into heaven without passing through death first. That makes me kind of unusual here. I still have my natural human curiosity, something angels don't have. I like to find out about stuff no one else up here worries about.

I have something very special to tell you about today.

It was just one week before the very first Christmas. For a long time, every week, the angel choir would gather together for a special rehearsal.

Treble, the choirmaster, was getting increasingly concerned. No, angels don't get anxious in the same way we humans get. But mind you, everything's not harps and clouds in heaven like some preachers claim. In fact, when it comes to Christmas program rehearsals, there's not much new under the sun—or above it either. This was plain to see as I watched.

"Now let's try the chorus again!" Treble announced. "And this time sing it with a little more feeling!"

Treble raised his arms to conduct, cued the organ to hit the first chord. Down came his arms and out came the most beautiful music I have ever heard.

"Glo-o-o-o-o-ry to God

In the hi-i-i-ighest"

It was so wonderful. But it wasn't just a sound. I never heard a sound that you could weigh. Once—on earth—my cousin, Anna, sang a song that made me tingle. But this was different. I was glad it was a short chorus, because I couldn't even breathe. This was a ten-ton song! I just couldn't breathe...

But apparently it wasn't satisfactory to Treble,

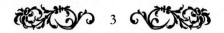

the choirmaster. Tap-tap-tap went the baton.

"Is that the best you can do? You sound like the Mormon Tabernacle Choir!" He was disappointed.

I didn't know what this "Mormon Tabernacle Choir" was, but later I found out that it represented high quality human music—far below what Treble expected of his angels.

Treble continued, "I want to be able to understand every word. We've only got one more week before the Christmas performance. You all should know the words by now. You've had since before the foundations of the earth to learn them! So get your heads out of your books and say each word clearly. We're going to be singing to some human shepherds, and they're going to be frightened enough as it is. It is essential that they hear the words clearly. It sounds to me like you're singing:

> *'lory to ah in the hi-a*
>
> *Pea on er goodwi to meh.*

Now is not the time to frighten these humans with some strange heavenly language. Pleazz ssspeaKCH KCHlearly. The word is 'peace' on earth, not 'pea' on earth. There's a big difference between the two you know!"

Treble urged one more time. "Let's try it again from the beginning with Michael's lines. This time I'm going to stand at the back of the galaxy. I want to be able to hear every word... Lights, are you ready? Organ?"

As Treble made his way to the back of the galaxy, I knew I'd better get out as quickly as I could. I didn't think I could bear a heavier sound.

❦

The words were still ringing in my ears as I walked the long hall toward my room. I didn't get far before I saw an angel, named Arbor, sitting in a corner in the Eastern Sky Lobby — all by himself. He seemed to be sad. But I wasn't sure, because it had been such a long time since I had seen that feeling in heaven.

Sure enough, Arbor was sad alright. For when I asked him what was the matter, out gushed the tears ... and the whole story.

"I just found out tonight (sniffle) that I'm not going to get to be (wail) in the Christmas Program (bawl!). And I can't go to the Christmas Party afterward."

"But why? What did you do?" I asked, thinking to myself, *How can an angel do anything wrong?*

"Nothing." Arbor hung his head. "All I know is (sniffle) that all the other angels get to go (wail) to the Christmas Program and Party (bawl!) but I don't. I'm supposed to take this (sniffle) silly box (which I don't know what's inside) and not supposed to open until midnight Christmas Eve in a small, barren field just outside of Jerusalem."

And with that, he held up the box for me to hold. It was wrapped in some kind of shiny green cloth, about the size of a lunch pail, tightly bound by a scarlet cord tied in a double knot so it wouldn't come open easily. It was very light. I shook it but heard nothing inside.

"Are you sure this isn't some kind of joke the other angels have dreamed up? I don't think there's anything inside."

"Oh yes (sniffle). I'm sure. I was summoned to God's Royal Throne Room where I was given the box and the instructions not to open it until midnight Christmas Eve right during the (sniffle) Christmas Program (wail) in a small, barren field just outside of Jerusalem, twenty miles away from (bawl!) all the other angels! (Sniffle) Why me?"

"Gee, Arbor. I don't know what to say. I'm sorry... but it must be important."

"Oh... I'm sure it is. (Sniffle) But why can't it wait a few hours? Why does it have to be opened right during the (wail) Christmas Program?"

"I don't know..." I paused. As I handed back the box, an idea struck me. "Say, Arbor. Did anyone tell you that you had to be alone when you open the box?"

"Well (sniffle)... no. But none of the other angels would pass up the (wail) Christmas Program to go with (bawl!) me. I asked."

"What about me? I could go with you. I can't go to the Christmas Program anyway. At least, I can't be too close. Twenty miles is a good, safe distance. What do you say? Do you want my company?"

"Why...sure! Would you really come along? That's great!"

Arbor's face turned all shades of happy. And, frankly, I was just as pleased knowing I would be a safe distance away from the heavenly host in concert. My all-too-human ears could not have taken another note of angelic exultation!

The week went by fast. There was so much for everyone to do. I found out that it was no small task to get a major production like this off the — or should I say — on the ground. Everything had to be timed perfectly to coincide with the star shining bright over Bethlehem.

Finally the night arrived. Everyone was excited and nervous. Small groups of angels were clustered in every corner rehearsing lines and cues with one another.

Then I saw Arbor coming down the hall toward me. He was terrific! Going up to one angel after another. Adjusting their wings. Picking lint off their robes. And saying things like, "Hang in there!" and "Don't forget those lines!" and "You'll do great! I want to hear you all the way in Jerusalem!" He sure was a different angel than the one I had seen a week ago.

Finally he came to me, "You know Enoch, I appreciate your going along with me. Just knowing I'm not going alone…"

I wanted to put my arm around his shoulder,

but we humans can't do that when an angel's happy. That is, not if we want to have an arm left.

So I just said, "You're welcome… Well, I guess it's time. You got the box? Let's go!"

In an instant we were in a small, barren field just outside of Jerusalem. To this very day, I don't understand how I get about. Of course, I did ask. But God lost me when He started talking about "molecular displacement." You've got to remember, when I went to school and the teacher said, "Get out your calculators," we all pulled out a bag of pebbles. All I know is this: you just think of where you want to be and, as long as it is where God wants you to be, you wind up there. Actually, that's sort of how it's supposed to be on earth, too, as it is in heaven.

The night was crystal clear and cold. I stood a little closer to Arbor and warmed my hands. Neither of us said very much. We waited for the cue to open the box.

The box! In all the hustle of Christmas preparations, my curiosity was left taking a winter's nap. But now I couldn't take my mind off of it. What could be inside? What could be so important? Why

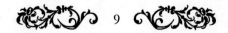

does it have to be opened on Christmas Eve night? I couldn't wait to see inside. If I had been wrapped up as tightly as that box, I would have burst my bows!

Just then, we heard the angels sing.

"Glo-o-o-o-ry to God
In the hi-i-i-ighest."

They did great! From twenty miles away you could hear every beginning and ending. Every "guh" and every "duh" and every "st."

"Open it! Open it!" I said.

Arbor was a little more patient, but even he tore the shiny green cloth as he worked. Underneath the cloth was a plain wooden box. That was no surprise. We guessed that by feeling it.

"Open it! Open it!" I said again.

Arbor lifted the hinged lid slowly and peeked inside.

"Let me see! Let me see!"

There was a note on top. Arbor picked up the note and read…

"Hello Arbor and Enoch. I'm glad
both of you are here tonight. It is quite
appropriate to have an angel and a man

performing my little service tonight. Rest assured that your help and sacrifice will not go unrewarded. There will be a Christmas party in your heart when you have finished your task. Now, proceed to the scroll which you will find in the box and follow the instructions carefully. And once again ... Thank you very much. It was for a time such as this that I created you. I'm glad you could make it."

Arbor reached inside the box. Sure enough— there was a scroll. It was plain and simple, like the box.

"Open it! Open it!"

Arbor grabbed the scroll in two hands and unrolled it. A small leather pouch fell out onto the ground. But neither of us touched it, since we were not told to do that yet.

"What's it say? What's it say?!" Again Arbor read:

"Tonight is a very special night indeed,
Open the pouch and then proceed."

"Open it! Open it!" I grabbed the pouch and handed it to Arbor.

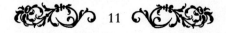 11

"You open it, Enoch. You're the one in such a hurry!"

"Me? Open it?" Somehow, the task became bigger than just opening a leather pouch. My fingers tingled as I pulled at the leather strings wrapped around the neck of the pouch. (And something began to happen in my heart.)

There didn't seem to be anything inside. I poked in one finger to feel around. Nothing.

"Tip it over and shake it," Arbor whispered.

"I did just that, but nothing came out... except... a tiny seed.

"Is this it?" I asked.

"I don't know. Let me keep reading:

"By now, of course, you've
  found the seed
That and your hands
    are all you'll need.
Place the seed in a hole in
    the ground.
Then cover with dirt,
    make a two-inch
    mound."

Arbor and I shared the task. He made the hole,

and I scraped up a handful of dirt. We buried the seed. As best I could measure, I measured the mound. Two finger knuckles high—one finger knuckle equals about one inch.

"Read on, Arbor." Arbor read:

> "Now you've completed
> your one Christmas
> task,
> And surely you're left with
> questions to ask.
> A good explanation is all
> that you'll need,
> And one you'll receive
> as you go on to read.
> Tonight in the City of
> David, you see,
> A baby is born—
> that baby is Me.
> I've come in the flesh,
> not to undergo birth
> Or scratch some old itch to
> live on the earth.
> I've come in the flesh just
> to die for men's sin

To clean out their hearts,
    so that I can come in.
My blood must be shed on
    a cross finally
And for that it is crucial to
    plant Me a tree.
A tree that is sturdy,
    but not too old,
A thirty year tree is good
    I am told
For making strong crosses
    that bear lots of weight,
For heavy are sins like envy
    and hate.
So what could be finer to
    do on this night
Than plant My own cross—
    keep My death in plain
    sight.
I wish I could be there,
    a 'Thank You,' I'd say,
But it happens just now I'm
    asleep in some hay."
That was it. Our task was done. Neither Arbor

nor I spoke. But just as God had promised, something filled our hearts with such joy we had never known.

And Arbor never, ever said anything to anyone about missing the Christmas Program and Party.

❦❦❦

Now, I don't know if the events of that night have anything to do with the traditions that have grown up around Christmastime. But I find it very interesting (and very much in tune with God's way of making everything fit together whether people recognize it or not) — I find it very interesting that it has become the practice in much of the world that fathers and mothers and little children, during Christmastime, go out into the fields and cut down a tree and bring it into their homes. At the very time when people are remembering that Jesus was born in a little manger in Bethlehem, in the middle of their homes stands a copy of the tree that God had planted which was to be cut down to make a cross for Jesus to die on.

And I find it very interesting that beneath that tree are placed wrapped boxes, tightly tied with paper cords, called ribbons, and bows. And inside those boxes are secret signs of love that people can't wait to discover.

I don't know about you, but I've never been able to look at a Christmas tree with shiny wrapped presents beneath without wondering, "Are all traditions really man-made?"

WHY BELLS ARE RUNG AT CHRISTMASTIME

Of course you know the names Joseph and Mary, Jesus' parents. Many of you have probably been one of them in some kind of Christmas program. They are very famous around Christmastime.

But, I'll bet you didn't know that there was another Joseph and Mary who lived in Jerusalem at the time Jesus was born, only ten miles away. They are not nearly so famous as Jesus' parents, but you really must hear their story.

It was the first Christmas Day. Jesus was just a few hours old, still well-swaddled and quiet in the manger. The shepherds had gone back to their sheep. And that was it for the first Christmas Day. No presents were exchanged. No fancy dinners with strange kinds of jello that you don't know what's in it. Nobody strung lights, or decorated cookies, or hung stockings—because most people didn't find out until many years later what had happened that night in Bethlehem.

But, of course, God knew. He had planned it all. And He was continuing to observe Christmas all week long. Many other people around the world got to unwrap His presence that week; they just didn't know it at the time.

And I got to watch some of them.

For example, as I said, it was Christmas Day. There was a marketplace in Jerusalem. A very busy place, where people used to buy and sell things right out in the streets in front of their own houses. House after house displayed tables piled with wares. Baskets hung from poles, ropes stretched between them bearing the weight of hundreds of belts and sandals. Colored cloth draped the tables stacked with clay pots upon clay pots. Squawking chickens clacked against wood slat cages. It was a noisy place.

I suppose I should remind you that the streets were very narrow. There were no sidewalks. Not a single house had a front yard, so when you opened your front door, you were at the shopping mall. It was a very noisy place.

Nothing had price tags. People were shouting out prices, "Sandals are 17 drachmas!"

But nobody ever accepted the first price, so they shouted back, "You're crazy!"

So the seller yelled back, "17 drachmas, not a penny less!"

"You're not serious, you thief. I saw one just like it at Levinson's for 15!"

"Then go to Levinson's! See what I care! You're the thief... taking food out of my little one's mouth!"

It was a very noisy place. And what made it even noisier were the sounds coming out of Zelda Hallmartz's house.

(Wail sound.) She was a professional mourner.

(Wail sound.) She was practicing.

(Wail sound.) In those days when someone died, the family showed their love, not by sending flowers to the funeral, but by paying for some women to

come and bawl their eyes out for four-to-five hours.

(Wail sound.) And Zelda Hallmartz was very good. *(Wail sound.)* Like I said, she practiced.

Zelda hadn't been in business very long, either. But in six short months, she had made a major splash in Jerusalem and built a very good reputation.

For one thing, she made a very smart business move by finding a home on one of Jerusalem's busiest streets. She lived there...*(Wail sound)* and practiced. People noticed.

Mostly she was a brilliant advertiser. Nobody had ever advertised professional mourners before. But Zelda had nerve...*(Wail sound)* and she practiced. Her reputation spread.

"You want someone good, get Zelda Hallmartz. She's good!" People spread the word.

Actually, to say she was an advertising genius is an understatement. She was the first person in history to send out calendars every year with **"Hallmartz Professional Mourners"** printed in bold. She was the first person to place hand-held fans in all the synagogues. So, in those hot summer months, while the teachers of the law were reading from Deuteronomy, people all over would be reaching for the fan and reading, *"Hallmartz Professional Mourners — We cry over anything, even spilt milk."*

Zelda believed in adding a little humor to an otherwise morbid occupation.

Oh, she had nerve. It takes nerve — day in and day out — to cry like you lost your own mother over someone you never met... and worse, someone you didn't even like.

But she practiced... and had the nerve to advertise. Some people (particularly the other professional mourners), thought it rather crude to advertise. But then "some people" didn't have the fastest-growing business in the marketplace.

Zelda even figured out — get this — a way to make the sign over her shop shine at night. What a genius! Remember — they didn't have electricity back then. So when it was dark — it was dark — and business life totally shut down for the night. But Zelda was not the sort to be beaten by the dark. She made it work for her. She thought, "When it's dark, anything bright shows up all the better!"

Suddenly, the darkness presented her advertising mind with enormous possibility... If only she could come up with a way to cast light on her sign. And she did.

First, she took the sign off her door frame, and elevated it above the rooftop. Then she tied ropes to two oil lamps and hoisted them up to the top of two tall poles on either side of her sign. She tied a cross-piece between the two poles up near the top, which gave her something to attach two mirrors to. The shiny side of the mirror pointed toward the sign. It was brilliant—but simple. The mirrors blocked the light coming toward people's eyes, while at the same time, reflected it toward the sign.

So, here on this dark street, in the middle of the marketplace, when all the other businesses were silent, shining out for all to see was her business name up in lights:

HALLMARTZ PROFESSIONAL MOURNERS
When You Care Enough
To Send The Very Depressed

Zelda had nerve, business savvy. But she was good— because why? She practiced.

That may be one reason God chose her to be involved in unwrapping His "presence" this first

Christmas Day in Jerusalem. If the most you can do is cry for a living, then do it your very best. And Zelda did.

That's why she was practicing this day. She was practicing and talking through the window to her friend, Francine DeMarco. Francine owned the basket shop right next door.

(Wail sound.) "Was that any better, Francine?" Zelda inquired between chomps on her gum. By the way, she chewed it for business purposes, as you'll see later. It was not a bad habit.

"You know *(chomp-chomp)*, Francine," Zelda continued, "I've cried at *(chomp-chomp)* almost every kind of funeral by now, but *(chomp-chomp)* this will be my first *(chomp-chomp)* child-funeral. I just feel like it *(chomp-chomp)* deserves a new kind of *(chomp-chomp)* cry. What do you think? Huh?"

The noise in the street made it very hard for Zelda to hear Francine's comment.

"A little break in my voice?" she asked. Francine nodded. "Let's see… a little break in my voice. O.K. Listen to this!"

(Wail — with break in voice.) "How's that? Pretty good?" she yelled. Francine shouted another sug-

gestion. "Say what? Make my shoulders shake? O.K. I'll give it a try."

(Wail—with break and shaking shoulders.) "What about that? I'd say that was pretty good!" Zelda looked for a nod of approval, and was perturbed at getting more suggestions from, of all things, a basket maker. "Two sharp screams and then repeat the shoulder shaking? Is that it? Really, Francine, I'm only getting 30 drachmas for this one. I don't want to ruin my voice...Yes, I know it is a special case... All right, but this is all, no more suggestions please! Let's see, you said a break in my voice, shaking shoulders, two sharp screams and back to shoulders shaking..."

(Wail, break, shoulders shake, two screams, shoulders shake.)

Francine approved and went back to arguing customers into buying her baskets. In this mall, the customer's always wrong. And Zelda kept practicing, not too much though. She had to save her voice for the funeral that night.

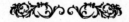

Ah yes, now that brings me to the funeral, and

the other Joseph and Mary I mentioned earlier. Unfortunately, on the very night Jesus was born— their son, Jacob, died. That's the way things go. The minute you're having your best fun, someone else in the world is having their worst hurt. You must never forget that.

The other Joseph and Mary were not taken by surprise when Jacob died. Two weeks earlier, his little body grew very hot, and the white spots began to appear on his neck and chest. Right then, they knew. And that very night, Joseph made his first lonely trip to the tomb he had been hewing out of the rocky wall just west of Jerusalem.

In those days, people were buried in tombs, caves carved into the rock walls. When finished, there was enough room inside for several bodies to be laid on flat surfaces, like big rock couches shoved against the inner walls of the cave.

From time to time, Joseph would go to the tomb he had chosen for his family and pick away at the rock walls inside. One day it would be his burial place. He needed to get it ready gradually, but there was no hurry, of course. He was only twenty-eight. So, he never worked at it too hard. Maybe once a month he'd pound and pick for a couple of hours and then head home.

Never did he expect that the first body to use the tomb would be his son's.

So the first night young Jacob fell ill, and the spots came, Joseph picked up his tools, walked through the streets of Jerusalem to the cave area, and set to work. Night after night, he carved his questions into the rough rock walls.

"Why, Lord? *(Beat-beat)* He is only seven years old. *(Beat-beat)* Is there nothing You can do?" *(Beat-beat)*.

But his prayers crumbled in piles of rubble at his feet, leaving only angry questions scarring the hard, unmoving walls of the tomb. Oh! He beat against those walls. But the harder he beat, the more the walls rang back the echoed taunt:

> **You beat, beat, beat against death**
> **To give life more room**
> **You beat, beat, beat against death**
> **And get only a bigger tomb!**

After one week, Joseph was nearly finished and he knew the time was drawing near. So on his last tomb digging trip, he stopped in at Zelda's (he'd seen the sign lit up) and requested her services. He wanted to give his son the best.

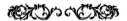

So now here it is Christmas Day. Jacob is one day dead. And Zelda arrived at dusk. Many people had already gathered in the other Joseph and Mary's home, ready for the long hike through the streets of Jerusalem to the tomb.

Zelda spotted Joseph and sidewaysed herself through the crowd to speak to him. "I'm so sorry, sir *(chomp-chomp),*" she said, still chewing her gum (for business purposes only, remember).

Her expression of sympathy drew a hollow nod from Joseph.

"I was wondering," she tried to whisper, "if you would *(chomp-chomp)* like me to weep quietly while we are *(chomp-chomp)* here at the house. Then my plan is to get *(chomp-chomp)* louder as we approach the tomb. Is that O.K.?" She tried to make eye contact.

"That's fine," Joseph nodded again. You could tell, as far as Joseph was concerned, nothing about the whole matter was fine. But since nothing could

change, anything was fine. Fine. "Fine," he repeat-
ed. "That'll be fine."

Zelda was disappointed in his reaction and sub-
tly objected to his apathy toward her sympathy by
making sure he was aware that her services were
not those of any run-of-the-mill professional
mourner.

"I've worked up a very special package for your
son. I'm sure when the pain has worn off, you'll
have fond memories of how well we mourned your
son's death."

Joseph's eyes let go of two tears. The left eye
dripped first, while the tear in the right held on just
a little longer before it, too, finally gullied down his
cheek. He thought, "There's more mourning in
those two tears than you have in...in..." He turned
away to find Mary's hand.

Zelda adjusted her hair, shifted her gum (which
she chewed strictly for business purposes) to the
upper side of her mouth so she wouldn't choke,
and began the first part of her program—quiet sob-
bing.

*I hope they appreciate that they are getting all the
frills at my no frills price,* she thought, reminding her-

self of her generosity. And while her mind drifted off, she became the channel of grief for the gathered crowd.

Before too long, it was time for the crowd to squeeze out of the house into the street and head for the tomb. There were hundreds of people. The funerals of children are quite popular, so everyone had turned out—from poor to rich, from uneducated shepherds to the wisest men. And in the very center of this mournful, moving congregation, born at about shoulder level, was the dead boy's body, swaddled in graveclothes.

Zelda's crying really stirred the crowd, and by the time they were passing her shop and the lighted sign, she felt a strong surge of pride in her business, her reputation, and another job well-done.

Perhaps she had done her job too well, because the wailing of the crowd (inspired, of course, by her program), had intensified to the degree that Zelda had to start her special cry sooner than expected in order to be heard above the sounds of the amateurs.

At first the cry didn't come naturally. She had to think it through. (*Wail, break, shoulder shake, two screams, shoulder shake.*) But by the time they arrived at the tomb, she wasn't having to concentrate at all.

The tomb. This was the part Zelda loved and hated at the same time. She got to go inside with the family. None of the crowd was important enough. She loved that. But then again, she had to be right in there—closer than she really wanted to be to the real grief and horror of the last, last contact between parents and child.

She bent down to go inside, but briefly paused, postponing another loud custom wail, while she took out her gum, pulled it in half, and without anyone noticing, placed a half-wad in each ear. Wailing inside hollow tombs day after day put many mourners into early retirement—moan deafness. Zelda took precaution.

Now what happened next may be hard for you to believe.

Joseph and Mary were finishing the final adjustment of the boy's body. Inside were three other family members, and Zelda. Zelda was in the middle of the shoulder shaking part of her customized wail, the crowd outside could hear it ringing, when all of the sudden…she screamed. Not the prepared scream, not the carefully practiced scream. She totally departed from her planned program and let out a terrible scream.

Everyone stopped. Heads peeked in the tomb. Joseph and Mary turned toward her — disgusted. *A mourner should remain in the background — always! This was totally uncalled for. Another advertising gimmick?*

No...Zelda had heard a voice speaking to her. But whose? Her shoulders drooped as her eyes lifted into a timid apology. *Hadn't anyone else heard?* She pulled the gum out of her ears and listened. Nothing.

She looked at Joseph, then lowered her eyes in repentance. Satisifed that there would not be another such outburst, Joseph and Mary turned back to the boy's body. Zelda put the gum back in her ears to resume wailing. Again...a voice! This time Zelda stifled herself and did not scream. But immediately she reduced her custom wail to a whimper. Her eyes darted back and forth in the dim light scanning the tomb for some explanation. Then the voice again! She heard words clearly, but no one else did — apparently.

"Zelda, in a moment this boy is going to sit up and begin to speak. He will live again. When that

happens, you must speak to the boy's mother and father."

Zelda's mouth froze open in a silent scream. The voice continued. **"Don't worry what to say. The words will come quite easily when it's time."**

Zelda began backing toward the tomb's entrance, ready to run.

"Zelda, it's too late. You've been chosen. Look, the boy's foot twitched."

Zelda's scream was about to break out. "Please!" she winced. Please what? She didn't know. Just please. It was time to say please. Whatever was about to happen, she didn't want to be there. Please.

The boy's chest rose and sank. The edge of the scream squirted out. Still no one else seemed to see it happen. She rubbed her eyes. It happened again! And again! And again! She screamed. The others saw. Mary gasped and burrowed into Joseph's chest. He wrapped his arm around his wife and edged forward reaching slowly for the cloth that covered the boy's face, and pulled it back.

His eyes were open! He said, "Mama?"

Mary wailed in uncontrolled, confused joy. What

a wail! For a moment, Zelda's professionalism locked in on that wail. "That was a good one. I can use that some other time," she admired.

But immediately words started flowing out of her mouth. As they came, she was actually thinking, *Zelda, dear, I know you have nerve, but this is going much too far.* But she couldn't stop herself. Here's what she spoke:

"This is what our Heavenly Father says:

You beat, beat, beat against death

To give his life more room.

You beat, beat, beat against death

And get only a larger tomb.

I beat, beat, beat against death

And a merry exchange I make

I beat, beat, beat against death

Your son's tomb for My Son, I'll take."

At that, Jacob sat up. His father and mother could hardly breathe as they stared. But then you should have heard the shouting! Joseph, Mary, Zelda, everyone screamed and wailed with joy. "He's alive! Alive! Alive! Alive! My son!" Such noise was never heard as it came echoing, ringing, peeling out of the tomb over the entire city of

Jerusalem.

Of course, Jacob was not quite sure what to make of it all and wondered what he was doing wrapped up in a cave.

About thirty-two-or-three years later, this same Joseph heard a man teach in Jerusalem, a man who did wonderful things for people and said He was the Son of God. Joseph watched and wondered. And he believed this man. God's Son. And waited and watched.

One day, they took this man and hung Him up to die on a cross. He died. And while all His disciples stood by motionless in horrified dismay, Joseph knew exactly what to do.

Having already obtained permission from the authorities, he carefully took the body of God's Son down from the cross. It was dark. There were no shepherds and wise townspeople this time, no Zelda. And on this deserted Friday night, Joseph of Arimathea once again carried — this time not his son but — the Son of God on his shoulders, through the streets of Jerusalem to that familiar site, where he wrapped God's Son in swaddling clothes and laid Him in the tomb, saying, "Beat, beat, beat against death. The merry exchange is made."

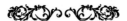

Now, I have to tell you, that no matter where I am at Christmastime, if I hear the sounds of bells, big bells, big round hollow bells, with that one lonely metal ball beating, striking against the hard, hard iron on the inside wall of the hard, hard bell—I can't help but think of Joseph beating, and his nighttime sorrows, and Zelda's dreadful custom mourning turned to shouts of joy ringing out over the city on the first Christmas Day.

Beat, Beat, Beat Against Death
A Merry Exchange I'll Make
Beat, Beat, Beat Against Death
Your Tomb For My Son, I'll Take

WHY JESUS
WAS BORN
IN A MANGER

H ello. Enoch here again. Back another year to give you the human interest angle on heavenly affairs. This year, I have a new story to tell.

As I understand it, for centuries, people have been intrigued with the fact that Jesus had to born in a lowly stable for animals. He was not born like all of you in a nice, clean room. Because at that time in Bethlehem, there were no "nice, clean rooms" left. All of them were filled. Every hotel and travel lodge, every wayside inn and boarding house, even the no-tell motels were filled up with people.

Preachers have always made a big deal about that.

"And so... there was no room for baby Jesus. No room for a poor young family. No room for an innocent and precious young maiden to have a child. No room for the Savior of the world to be born. Nowhere for Him to lay down His sweet head!"

Like I say, they always made a big deal about it. Then they go on to say,

"No, there was no place for Jesus Christ to be born except a lowly, filthy, smelly, flea-infested, ragtag, ramshackled, dilapidated, old animal stall! The Savior of the world in a mangy manger!"

Preachers often get carried away. I've never met a kid yet who doesn't like to play in the hay in cow barns—as long as it's not the kind that sticks together. So I can't really imagine Jesus minding being laid in a manger too much. But these preachers get carried away painting "word pictures," trying to get everyone to see how awful it was, and that **"this is just like the world is today. People still don't have room for God."**

Poppycock! Need I remind you that if God had

wanted for Jesus to be born in the finest hotel room in Bethlehem— there would have been plenty of room. It had nothing whatsoever to do with the world being too full to make room for God. God chose not to have Jesus born at a hotel, motel, or any-tel-at-all. So lets get down off this picky-pokey attitude about how mean the world was to Jesus. It is quite unbecoming to the Christmas spirit. Anyways, they didn't know that the little, round ball inside of Mary's womb was Jesus. If they had known it was Jesus, they would have made room for Jesus, because anybody who really knows Jesus just loves having Him close by.

It's definite. Jesus was born in a manger, because God wanted it that way. Of course, the big question is "why?" And that's what I'm going to answer this year. Why was Jesus born in a manger?

I can answer that question in three words. Thaddeus Ben Thaddeus. He was one of the most unforgettable persons I have ever met. And he was why Jesus was born in a manger.

Thaddeus Ben Thaddeus. He went by T. Ben

Thaddeus. Owner of Southside Livery Stable. Sounds important... But the kids called him "T-bone." T-bone Thaddeus. I'll bet I don't even have to describe T-bone Thaddeus to you. After all, anybody kids call "T-bone" can only look one way. Skinny! Tall and SKI-I-I-NY.

Every single bone in his nineteen year old body pushed as far out of his skin as it could, just to let everyone know, "He's skinny."

Everything sticking out of his body was exactly the same size around. His legs, arms, wrists, neck — all measured the same — 6 inches around. If he ever would've gotten his leg cut off below the knee, you could've just sewn on somebody else's arm in its place. Nobody would've ever known the difference — provided he didn't wear open-toe sandals. Anyways — you get the picture. T-bone Thaddeus was skinny.

On top of his skinny body and neck, balanced his face. Poor Thaddeus. He had a big nose that apparently did not know the meaning of the words, "Stop growing!" He had three big front teeth and two ears that must have thought they were in some sort of competition with the nose — *who can get the farthest away from the face.* But I don't blame them. He had the kind of face that makes anybody want to get away — far away.

On top of that, T-bone couldn't speak very well either. His three big teeth often got in the way. He tried to keep them out of sight behind his upper lip, because he was so embarrassed about them. So he mumbled a lot. And yet — those big teeth still fell out in plain view any time he said the "th" sound. And you just can't go around leaving out words that use the "th" sound. That would mean you couldn't say fa**th**er or mo**th**er, **th**ank you, or even his own name. Poor **Th**addeus.

Poor, poor T-bone Thaddeus. He hardly ever left his house. Walking out anywhere in public was sort of like throwing fresh meat to a pack of wild dogs. Or worse, like throwing one Barbie doll to a gaggle of giggly first grade girls. People were unkind to him, and the kids were worst of all. They used to make fun of him every time they saw him. They even made up a jump rope song about him:

> **T-bone Thaddeus**
> **Looks so baddeus**
> **Won't you please stay home.**

Or—your ears could grow
Then your face won't show
And that will make us gladdeus.

Is it any wonder that T-bone Thaddeus enjoyed being with animals more than people? After all, the animal kingdom is exactly the place where God experimented with noses, ears, and teeth in all sorts of strange combinations and sizes until he finally came upon the arrangement that would look best on a human being. Poor Thaddeus. But he sure did feel more at home among the animals. He loved tending his three cows, four sheep, two chickens, five dogs, a cat, and one goat. But he did not love people. He didn't even like talking to people or anything.

No one was welcome at his house. He had no friends. And should a stranger chance to come to his door, T-bone Thaddeus would not answer.

"Hello... Hello... Anybody there?... I say, Anybody there?"

T-bone Thaddeus just could not open the door and face that first instant when the person on the other side saw what Thaddeus looked like. Most people would look quickly at the ground. Some even broke out laughing, but then quickly apologized, saying something about having just remembered a good joke. But they never fooled T-bone. He knew—he was the joke. His skinny body and big nose, two big ears, and three big teeth made them laugh.

You can see why T-bone Thaddeus soon learned to spend most of his time out in his stable with his animals. That's why it's no surprise that that's where God's angel found T-bone Thaddeus the weekend before Jesus' birth.

T-bone was in the middle of combing down one of his cows, when the angel appeared—half-floating, half-sitting about one foot off the ground.

"Fear not!" the angel announced majestically, as he put out his hand as if to touch the top of T-bone's head. T-bone hardly looked up from his cow. "So who's afraid?" he wondered.

"You are supposed to be afraid. You're supposed to be shaking and trembling with fear, falling on your face and everything. That's what it says right here in my training manual—chapter 9, section 4, paragraph 1—and I quote:

'When breaking into the earthly realm and into the presence of human beings, all messenger angels must first say, "Fear not," since human beings react to all supernatural events with terror and disbelief.'

Unquote. Now I am an angel, correct? And unless I'm mistaken—you are a human being, are you not?"

T-bone Thaddeus stopped combing his animal friend. His arms drooped to his side. "Theoretically, yes. But it's hard to be sure, because I've never been treated like a human being."

"Well," thought the angel and responded, "now you are, because God has a message for you."

"What could God possibly have to say to me?"

"Listen, do you want to be treated like a human being or not?"

"I don't think I know how."

"Just listen and do what God says, and you'll be all the human being He expects you to be."

"O.K. I'm listening."

"All right then. Let's take it from the top."

The angel opened up his small scroll and began

to read, "Fear not!... A-hem...uh...oh we already covered that. Let's see. Here we are...

'The God of heaven and earth
Wishes your presence at His birth.
And if you are able
Please lend Him your stable.

In just one short week
A man and woman will seek
A place in the town
Where she can lie down.

The Lord has made sure
The only room will be here
For Him to be born
And hope to keep warm.

So when they arrive
Please let them inside
And give them a place
With just enough space.

For one father, a mother,
And new born boy

And the Savior of men
Will fill you with joy.'

That is God's message. Now arise and go in peace."

"Go in peace? I'm at home already."

"Well then....just...arise and I'll go in peace. Er—
a—you arise in peace and I'll just go." With that, the
angel turned to leave.

"Wait-wait-wait, wait, wait. The Savior of the
world is going to be born in my manger? Why?
Why me? Why my manger?"

The angel just shook his head. "I really don't
know. The best I can figure is—you're His type. But
the important thing is that it *is* going to happen.
And very soon, so be ready."

"Well—I'm not looking forward to the company,
but I'll be ready."

"Fine then. I shall leave you in peace."

Again the angel turned to float away, but then
paused with his back to Thaddeus. Finally spinning
around, he asked, "You quite sure you weren't just
a little afraid?" The pleading and hopeful tone in
his voice let Thaddeus know that he should admit to
at least a brief moment of uncertainty.

"You might call it momentary fright," he offered.

That seemed to help the angel. He was able to regain his composure.

"Fear not," he said once more, this time feeling much better about the world as it was supposed to be. So with a pleasant sense of accomplishment, the angel turned around and this time was gone.

Thaddeus hardly wasted a moment from that point on. A lot of work had to be done and in a short period of time. Just as the angel had foretold, a young woman on a donkey and a man stood outside his house at about 8:30 the next Saturday evening.

Thaddeus had done a good job preparing the stable for them. He even built a new manger by lashing together two crosspieces of old wood for legs, and setting a box between them, filled with fresh hay for the little soon-to-be-born baby boy. He was excited about his company, but it still took all the courage he could muster to open his door and let them see what he looked like. Nevertheless, he did.

They did not laugh. They did not even look away. They smiled. Both their smile and request were sincere and simple.

"Please, a place for us to have our child."

"Right <u>th</u>is way."

Thaddeus motioned toward the stable. He didn't even mind saying a "th" sound. He led them to the stable, pointed out the manger, and introduced them proudly to each of his animals. But it quickly became clear that the young girl needed privacy, so Thaddeus politely excused himself and went into his house.

At about eleven o'clock on that crystal-clear night, Thaddeus awoke to a new animal sound coming from his stable. It was a baby's cry. He felt drawn to see the baby. Babies have their problems with looks, too. Their bald heads are too big for their tiny bodies. They have no teeth at all and two fat, scrunchy cheeks which swallow up a poor excuse for a nose. T-bone Thaddeus liked babies.

He rushed to the stable; but as he turned the corner to enter, he saw that it was filled with strangers. Thaddeus was horrified. This wasn't in the angel's prediction.

That night he never did get a close look at the baby Jesus. He just waited all night in a shadow at the rear corner of the cattle stall.

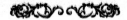

By now you may be asking, "Is that it? What does that have to do with why God chose the manger? And why that manger? And why was T-bone Thaddeus so unforgettable? Just because he was so funny looking?"

No. He was not so unforgettable because of his skinny body, big nose, two big ears, and three big front teeth.

Why a manger—that manger? Why the manger of T-bone Thaddeus? And why was he so unforgettable? I will answer all these questions—now.

You see, I never even really met Thaddeus personally, though I did see him face-to-face. And I never even talked to him, though I did hear him speak. Our paths crossed quite briefly while I was on assignment in Jerusalem some 50 years after the birth of Jesus in T-bone Thaddeus' stable. I was travelling with an angel friend when I saw Thaddeus and heard him speak. I was horrified! I asked this angel friend who he was. And, as I watched Thaddeus hanging, dying on a cross, my angel friend told me the story I have just told you, and that Jesus, some 30 years after His birth in T-bone Thaddeus' stable, went back to that stable to seek out Thaddeus and asked him to be one of His twelve apostles.

That's right. If you look in your Bibles, you will find the name "Thaddeus" listed right there among the more famous disciples, like Peter, James and John. That's right — the T-bone Thaddeus. The man who liked animals and shadows, but not people and conversation, became an apostle of the Light of the World, sharing the good news of salvation from the God who so deeply loved the world of people.

T-bone Thaddeus.

As my angel friend told the story — I just watched Thaddeus' face. I didn't laugh, or look away, or cry. There was no reason to. And just before he died, I saw him smile a great big smile. Sure enough, there were those three big teeth. But then he spoke these words that I will never forget:

> **"T-bone Thaddeus**
> **Doesn't look so baddeus**
> **Jesus, take me home**
> **Where my heart will grow**

And my face will glow

As long as you will daddy us."

With that, his head slumped forward. As we turned to leave, my angel friend paused with his back to Thaddeus. Then, as if recalling some old memory between friends, he spun around and called out in a whisper, "Fear not, T-bone Thaddeus. Arise and go in peace."

WHAT GOD
THINKS OF
SANTA

I was sitting in the outer chambers of God's Royal Hearing Room playing Chinese checkers with my angel friend, Ho-Feng. You may know him as Michael the Archangel. But angels are always blending into their surroundings in an attempt to be inconspicuous. And since we were playing Chinese checkers, Michael just naturally turned a little yellow, slanted his eyes, and politely asked to be called *"Ho-Feng"* for the duration of the game.

Well... there we were. I think Ho-Feng was about ready to turn back into Michael (if you know what I mean), when all of the sudden we both were startled to hear a great commotion echoing toward us down the alabaster corridor.

"Well, I think it's just disgraceful!" one angry, highpitched voice shouted.

"Disgraceful? Dis*graceful*!? How can anything so lovely, so loving, so positive, so effective, so influential, so…so…so good be disgraceful?!" came the other, much gentler sounding, voice.

"I'll tell you how." And with that, the angel Nomo—we all called him "The Old Lawyer"— began to wave wildly in one hand what appeared to be a pair of trousers, rather large, made of thick red flannel, and in the other hand a pair of brightly polished black boots. "Look at this *paraphernalia!'*

That's why we called him the old lawyer. He was always arguing fine points and using big words like *"paraphernalia."* I think you and I would just say, *"Stuff."*

"So what's wrong with a little old fat man wearing that par-a-phernalia?" That was Jonathan, the other principal in what appeared to be a very hot debate.

"What's wrong?!" Nomo nearly choked. "I'll

tell you what's wrong! Some little old fat man in a red suit is monopolizing too many people's attention... and not just children either. And the point is: Every bit of attention given to some little old fat man is a bit of attention taken away from God. That's what's wrong!"

"Oh, I see..." replied Jonathan. "So I suppose you want to burn down all the forests on earth, uproot all the flowers, defeather all the birds, paint the sky gray, and drain the colors from the rainbow—just so no one on earth will ever give their attention anywhere else than to God."

"No, no, no, no. I didn't say that. You can keep all those *things*, because God created them. If people give their attention to them, He gets their attention indirectly. This is different... This is a little old fat man. A little old fat *man*—not God. Man. Just another way those infernal wayward beings down there have come up with to focus attention on themselves rather than on God. Don't you see? This way they don't have to believe in God. They can just believe in some little old fat man who gives good little boys and girls lovely gifts. Well I think it's sick. The devil's trick—sick, I say. Sick!"

At this point there was a lull in the argument. By now, Nomo and Jonathan had drawn quite a crowd of spectators. Ho-Feng and I had suspended our game of Chinese checkers. The crowd was buzzing. Some agreed with Nomo. Others agreed with Jonathan. Still others were simply enjoying the entertainment. After all... there's not much excitement in heaven on the average day when celebration depends on whether Christians on earth are bringing people to salvation. It had been a dry week, so I guess for that reason some of the angels got a little out of hand trying to stir up some fun.

One of the angels slipped into the little old fat man's red flannel suit and black boots and began to taunt Nomo...all in good fun, of course.

"Come, little Nomo. Sit on Santa's lap. Tell me—have you been a good little angel?"

The crowd roared with laughter, but Nomo's face turned redder than Rudolph's nose.

"Alright, I've had it!... Do you really think it's alright for human beings—little impressionable human beings—poor innocent, misguided earthlings..." this was Nomo's best attempt at an emotional appeal. "Do you really think it is *right* for these young, potential believers to believe something that's not true, even to the point of making lists for Christmas and writing 'Dear Santa' letters, filled with nothing but selfish requests?"

"So, what's new with that? Seems to me like most prayers coming into heaven from adults are about the same," observed Jonathan.

"Well, at least they are praying to God and not to some little old fat man in a red flannel suit... O-i-o-eeenough of this! Let's just ask God!"

This brought a hush to the crowd. Someone yelled out, "Don't bother God with little questions like this!"

But Jonathan strode forward and knocked on the door to God's Royal Hearing Room. "If it's important enough to concern Nomo, it's important enough to concern God." And at that, the door to God's Royal Hearing Room opened.

From the doorway appeared a blinding light flooding into the already sparkling outer chamber. When the light died down, we all saw God standing in the doorway wearing His Royal Housecoat, His glasses pulled down to the tip of His nose. He was holding a notepad in one hand and a pen in the other.

"What can I do for you?" were His first words—they're always His first words. No one ventured even a syllable of sound. Everyone was a little embarrassed to bring up something so trivial.

"Well..." God prompted, "I am a patient person, but patience can run out. What seems to have brought you all here to My door? Nomo... does that red suit have something to do with this informal little congregation we have assembled here?"

Nomo stepped forward and cleared his throat—three times—before he finally managed to make his concern known.

"God, You know me." A simple statement of fact which brought a nod of assurance from God. So Nomo continued... "And you know that I am always concerned that You get as much attention as possible..." Again a pause, followed by a nod from God. "And whenever I see things that seem to take away from Your glory and worth—I just can't help from speaking up."

"Nomo—you never cease to amaze Me. If I were as concerned about My glory as you are—I could never have lived on that earth for even thirty minutes, not to mention thirty years. I wish you'd learn to let Me be the judge of things... But that's beside the point. What is it this time... specifically?"

"Well, God. I'm concerned about this Santa Claus fellow, alias St. Nicholas, alias Kris Kringle. He seems to be attracting the attention, not to mention the requests, of a goodly portion of human beings. I'm concerned that Your birthday celebration has been overshadowed by this little old fat man. I'm concerned about all these poor young earthlings who actually believe that at Christmastime they are visited by some jolly old elf who fills their stockings with toys and treats. I'm concerned about how disappointed they are when they find out that this little old fat man is a fraud, a department store phoney, *and* when they don't get everything they asked for. I'm concerned..."

"Nomo — that's quite enough. I get the idea. I wasn't born yesterday, you know. Here's what I think. I think... let it be. That's what I think."

The crowd stirred.

"Let it be?... Let it be! That's no answer," argued Nomo. "Is it right? Or is it wrong? That's what I want to know. Will you let it continue, or will you put a stop to it?"

"Nomo, I said *let it be*. Why do you have to make everything right or wrong? Can't you just let some things be? Let it be."

And with that God turned and walked back into His Royal Hearing Room. The excitement was over. Nomo was miffed. Jonathan puzzled. Everyone was quiet.

Ho-Feng had turned back into Michael in all of the excitement. He said he did not feel like finishing our game of Chinese checkers, and went to take a nap. Soon the outer chambers were deserted, and I was all alone.

Then I noticed that God had left the door to His Hearing Room slightly ajar. I've always been a curious fellow. When I see an open door, I walk in.

So I did. I walked into the Royal Hearing Room. No angel would ever have walked in uninvited. But we're built differently. And I walked in... very slowly of course.

❧❧❧ ❧❧❧

The room was dark except for the dim burning oil lamp on God's study desk. I made my way quietly toward the desk and behind it to the great swivel chair made of the very wood from Noah's Ark.

I sat down. It was still warm. "God must have just left the room," I whispered. "Imagine me, sitting in God's chair, behind God's study desk..."

And then I saw it. Laying on the desk—open for anyone to read—was the book...God's Diary. I figured if I weren't supposed to read it, He would have taken more care to lock it up. But there it was, open to that very day's page. I would never have touched the Diary or flipped back to any page. But there it was—already open. All ready to be read. So I read it.

To this day I have never forgotten the few words written there by God's own left-hand:

Dear Diary,

Some of the angels were upset today. They think my idea of Santa Claus is a bad idea. They wouldn't say so if they knew that it was my idea. They just don't understand me. Who does? That's why Santa is so important. Without his help, there would be many people who could never imagine that

there could ever be a person whose chief joy
came in giving good gifts to children. But if
they can believe it about a little old fat
man—*especially* when they are young—
they will be more likely to come very, very
close to believing and understanding me.

Just a little understanding. That's what I
want. If I could come to the world as a help-
less little burping baby so that people could
know me, then surely I can let some little
old fat man at the North Pole represent me.

I don't know how long I stayed there reading
those words. Finally I came to my senses and decided I had better leave. But just as I swung around in
the swivel chair to leave, there was God. He'd been
there all the time. My face must have turned all
shades of white. But God smiled and said gently,
"You may leave now, Enoch."

And then I knew. He had intended for me to
walk in that door. He had left the oil lamp burning
dim. He had left His personal Diary open to that
day's entry for me to read.

I began to leave quietly, but just as I reached the
door to go out of the Royal Hearing Room, God

spoke these words, "Enoch, do you understand me?"

I nodded...sort of. And then He said, "I'm glad you came. There are answers. For all good questions, there *are* good answers. Good night, Enoch. And please close the door on your way out."

WHY GOD
LIKES IT QUIET
AT CHRISTMAS

G od was sitting on His throne in heaven with His elbows on the long ivory supper table, His head in His hands. He was disgruntled. An angel by His side was asking, "Why can't You just change the rules?"

"Because I can't," He replied. "That's just the way things are. Once I make things one way there's no turning. And I made people a certain way. For some reason now, whenever they come near me in prayer, they talk, talk, talk. They feel they have to tell Me about themselves—as if I don't already know."

"Oh, I guess they can't help it. But I can't help it either. I just have that effect on them. Maybe it's the way I look... this big old gaudy crown. And I never have been satisfied with My hair and bushy old beard! It hides My mouth everytime I smile, unless, of course, I laugh. But then all the buildings shake and the clouds tear. And we lose a few more angels. Goodness knows, we can't afford to lose any more. There's work to be done: filing incoming prayers after I answer, numbering hairs, watching sparrows in case they fall, and... wait a minute. Here comes a prayer."

A prayer echoed in God's chamber.

"And, O God, have mercy on me, Lord. Out of your loving-kindness, forgive me, please Lord. I know that I am a terribly sinful person, and my heart is desperately wicked. My tongue is always lashing out against my fellow man, and my hands are too quick to hurt. O Lord, only You can forgive me. Please. Amen."

When the prayer was over, God resumed His complaint.

"There—you see? They're doing it again. Talk, talk, talk. Telling me all about their hearts, and tongues, and hands. Oh—I'm not mad at them. But why? Why do they act like that? Why?"

And God put His elbows on the long ivory supper table again and shook His head.

Just then, a little angel peeked around the edge of the table and said very shyly, "Uh—God? I believe I know why people act like that. You know, Your power is greater than any power on earth. And Your light—why, it is brighter than all the suns of the universe put together. And fair? You're so fair that every suppertime You know how to divide apple pie among 6000 angels so that everybody gets exactly the same-sized piece. Nobody on earth can do that. Not even mothers can divide a piece of pie in two so that their children don't argue.

"Your power, Your light, Your fairness. No one on earth can even understand You really. So every time You get involved, every time You insist on going down there to be with Your people, You're always doing something they don't understand. You talk from burning bushes. You cut a whole lake in half. You make food fall out of the sky. You blind people with Your light. You make walls fall down. You cause people to go deaf—and their faces to glow. People who walk suddenly limp. People who limp suddenly walk.

"People get scared... And then on top of that, they see how honest You are. Right gets rewarded. Wrong gets punished—eventually.

"Well, I'll tell you—I'm an angel so I've never been afraid. But I know a few human beings pretty well. And they get scared. And when they get scared, they usually start to talk—fast—because they are nervous."

"You mean they talk so much about themselves, because they're scared of Me?" God challenged.

"'fraidy cats, Lord."

"Scared?"

"...to death."

God stood up from His golden throne and walked slowly toward the great velvet curtains hanging behind the long ivory supper table. In one long, pensive motion, He pulled them back and looked out through the crystal picture windows toward the earth.

"Something's got to change," He said repeatedly. "Somethings's got to change. I don't want them coming to Me talking and talking and talking because they are afraid of Me. I want to be able to speak to them and have them listen without being shaken. I want them to be quiet and know that I am God — that I love people — I only hate evil — that I heal hurts — that I have their best interests in mind.

"They've got the wrong picture of Me. Something's got to change. Oh, I'd give anything to have just one human being come into My presence and be silent. No talking. Just listening. And learning what I'm really like. I'd give anything. Something's got to change..."

That next day was an especially long day. God just walked around heaven in a very unusual manner. He was fiddling with His crown, scratching His beard as He thought. He kept going back to those velvet curtains, looking out toward earth, drumming His fingers on the crystal window pane as He thought.

Then suddenly He turned. "Have the choirmaster begin rehearsals immediately. I will have need of the angelic choir." After further instruction, He motioned everyone out of the room. All of the angels floated out immediately and shut the heavy oak doors.

God walked slowly to His golden throne. Carefully, He took off His royal robe. Gently and very neatly—just like you'd expect Him to do it— He folded His robe and laid it on the long ivory supper table. Then He sat down and took off His crown and carefully laid it on His royal robe folded neatly on the supper table. A tear rolled down His cheek and landed on the crown. Instantly it turned into the brightest diamond you'd ever see on the very top of the crown.

Then He pushed back His golden throne—and stood up. He took off His royal slippers and set them down on the floor by the golden carved leg of His throne. There was God in heaven—standing— no crown, no robe, barefoot! With only a flimsy housecoat on!

He walked over to the great crystal window. It was nighttime on the earth now. The moon was glowing over to the right. God touched His finger to the crystal window, and a star—brighter than all the rest—made its way to a little spot over the earth.

As He went to close the great velvet curtains, He said, "Something's going to change. I want it quiet tonight in My presence."

He walked slowly to the outer door, the door that opens right out into the universe. He gave one last look around His royal chamber. The great velvet curtain. The long ivory supper table. His golden throne, His royal slippers, His royal robe folded neatly—just like you'd expect Him to do it—and the crown.

Then He turned off the lights and stepped out of the door.

That very night on earth, underneath the brightest star the world has ever seen, a little baby was born in a manger in Bethlehem. His parents were unusually quiet. The animals laid down in the hay together, but were not sleeping. A handful of shepherds came and knelt before the baby without speaking. Not a single person said a solitary sentence. It was perfectly quiet. And the baby smiled... then the angels sang:

"GLORY TO GOD IN THE HIGHEST. ON EARTH... PEACE AMONG MEN."

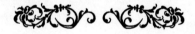

How God
Got Small

Hello—you should remember me by now. My name is Enoch. Every year I have this special opportunity to visit you and bring another glimpse of the heavenly events surrounding Christmas.

Since I never died before I was taken to heaven, I am every bit still human. As a normal man in heaven, I have had the privilege of participating in some of the most important events of all time. Since I am a man—not an angel—I think and wonder like you, and I know the kind of questions you want answers for.

So I come once a year—to satisfy your curiosity about Christmas events and traditions that have become so important in the world.

Today, it is my pleasure to tell you about the

most fascinating journey and battle of wits the world has ever known.

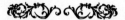

I'm sure you know that Christmas is the time we celebrate the birth of Jesus. And, I guess you also know that Jesus was like all babies—with soft, squishy flesh covering bones that hadn't decided whether or not to get hard yet.

But do you understand what I mean when I tell you that Jesus was God... IN-THE-FLESH? That means that all-of-God was in Jesus' body.

> *Squeezed into His fingers*
> *Curled around each heart's tick*
> *The God of creation*
> *Filled every cell's niche.*

The very God who used His mighty hands to mold the first man was pressed into hands that couldn't do a thing except twitch at loud noises.

Every bit of God was in every bit of Jesus. Every time Jesus' round little belly puffed up and out, and unpuffed in and down—God was there. Imagine—

> *The God of all breath*
> *Who wave-tossed the high seas*

Now barely had room
For even a sneeze.

The Lord of great knowledge
The God of all thought
Was tucked underneath
Jesus' fuzzy soft spot.

You know what the soft spot is, don't you? That's the place at the front top of a baby's head that parents say you must be very, very careful never to touch too hard. Sometimes they let you feel it—*gently*...! But once you do it, you don't really want to do it ever again anyway. Imagine—it's funny to think if you had touched Jesus' soft spot,

You would have been squishing
God, the Lord most sane,
Who Himself fashioned
And rationed the brain.

That's what it means to say that Jesus was God-in-the-flesh. Every bit of God was in every bit of Jesus.

But maybe now you're wondering how someone so big, such as God, could become someone so small, such as Jesus.

Well, that's the amazing story that I'm here to tell: How God became small. Now, I don't want you to get frightened as I tell this story, but it involves basically only two people. God and (you probably guessed it) Satan. Some people call him Lucifer, or the devil, but personally, I prefer to call him what Gabriel, the archangel, calls him every time he floats around outside of heaven's gate just to be a bother. Gabriel is notified and always drops whatever he is doing just to stand at the north gate entrance and yell, "Hello-o-o-o, Buffy."

Buffy! That makes Satan so mad! Satan wants to feel powerful, but to be called "Buffy" makes him feel as harmless as a pampered city kid at summer camp.

He's really not as harmless as the angels make him out to be. As this story will tell—and I don't want to scare you—God had quite a time. Because Satan (that's the name I'll keep using since you are more familiar with it)... because Satan fought him all the way. Here's how it happened.

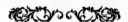

God stepped out of His Royal Chamber in heaven and faced the earth. In order to get to the earth, God really didn't have to move—or travel like you think of travel. All He had to do was get smaller, and He'd get closer.

Think of putting a marble at your feet. Right up against your toe. There's no way you can really move any closer, and it still seems far away to you, because it's way down at your feet. The only thing you could do to get any closer would be to get smaller. And the smaller you got, the closer to the marble you would get.

That's how God had to do it. The minute He stepped out of heaven, His toes went right up against the earth, but He was still a long way away. And He would be, until He started to get smaller.

Now—the only way God can get any smaller is to give up some of what makes Him so big. And that's what Satan tried to prevent Him from doing. God would have to get small enough not just to come to earth, but to find Mary, Jesus' mother, and get inside of her.

God was standing, looking down at the earth, when Satan, who is much smaller, began to buzz around God's ear.

"How in heaven — er — a — how in the world —
er — a — how in God's name — e — a — how in Jesus'
name — er — a — You're sort of caught out here in the
in-between zone aren't You, Big Fella? How are
You gonna get down there?"

God did not respond to the thing's buzz. "The
Thing." That's what God called Satan. Not Satan, or
Lucifer, or the devil, or even Buffy.

Names are big with God. And when Satan left
heaven, God took away his name. That's why we
have so many different names for Satan. He really
doesn't have one of his own. But to God he was just
a thing with no name.

Anyways, God did not respond. But Satan kept
right on, because he knew what many humans
don't know about God. He knew that even when
God doesn't seem to be paying attention, He really
is. So Satan kept on talking in faith that God was listening.

"You know I'm not about to let Your Royal
Highnie get down there — don't you? I know Your
plan. To become a person — die on the cross for
people's sin — my beautiful works of sin — and then
rise from the dead and defeat me. I know Your

plan. And right now You may be big and me small, but in order to get down there you've got to get small... smaller than me. And that's when I'm going to get You."

God smiled (Satan hated that smile) and blinked, almost knocking Satan clear to Jupiter. God thought, "I'm going to have to give up My muscles. My power. That'll get Me considerably smaller."

But just as God was about to say, **Let there be no muscles!** (that's the way God always gets things done) Satan whizzed past His ear on the way to earth hissing, "You'll be sorry..."

God watched Satan fly to earth penetrating its atmosphere leaving a trail of tornadoes in his wake.

The next thing He saw tore at His heart as if Satan himself was poking his twisted, pointy finger deep into it. Volcanoes erupted, melting people. Thatch-roofed homes caught fire dropping on young sleeping children. The earth quaked and swallowed; the rivers swelled and drowned; the diseases festered and killed.

God couldn't bear it any longer. "Enough! Peace!" And Satan stopped.

God's eyes burned with rage as the evil thing zoomed back to God's face.

"That's just a sample of what I'm going to do the minute You take off Your muscles. So go ahead—it's your decision. Don't let me pressure You. True...millions of people will be screaming out to You,

> *'God, if You're there*
> *If You care*
> *If You love us*
> *Up above us*
> *Won't You be fair?*
> *Save us — the lives*
> *That You gave us — please spare.'*

Don't let them pressure You though. Go ahead, give up Your power. It'll only be a million or two who will go to their graves cursing You for not helping."

Satan could feel the advantage in his position. He could feel himself expanding with pride and power he'd never known—growing larger and larger. At least, he thought he was getting bigger, but actually God was getting smaller. Satan was befuddled.

"I can't believe You're going to leave the earth, land and sea, unprotected from little old me. Why? I know for a fact that Your heart is breaking for those innocent little worms."

"My heart has even more breaking to do," was all that God said.

Satan flew away more determined now than ever to prevent God from getting inside Mary and becoming Jesus.

With all His great power pretty much gone—God was now about the size of the earth. He set out to find Mary. It didn't take long. Since God was as big as the earth, He could be everywhere on earth at the same time. He found her quickly. But once He found her, He knew that He must get smaller still by giving up His ability to be everywhere at once. He would have to give up His reach.

Can you imagine how difficult that would have been?

Think of all the things you are able to reach now. You can reach doorknobs and open the door all by yourself. One time you couldn't. You don't have to climb up on the counter to reach the cereal anymore. Maybe your feet can even reach the floor on the school bus. Imagine if you had to decide to get small again, and you couldn't reach all those things anymore.

Now think of God, Who can reach everything, having to decide to give up His reach. All those things He had gotten used to touching now would be beyond His reach if He got any smaller.

That was hard for Him, and Satan made it even harder. For just as God was about to say, **Let there be no reach!** Satan approached Him carrying a box.

"Here—open it. I made it for You."

God reluctantly took the box. He hated to touch it. After all, Satan's greasy, grimy hands, the ones that leave smudges wherever he goes, had handled the box. God opened the box and lifted out a small gold coin.

"Now, let me explain," jabbed Satan. "I know that Your power is gone, and that means You can only protect what You can cover. If You get any smaller You'll leave the world of people wide open for me—unprotected, uncovered. So I thought this little gold coin would be an appropriate gift. Because if You leave these people uncovered... just watch. Toss that gold coin down there between those two men — and don't touch them at all — don't hold them back. Just watch what will happen."

So God dropped the gold coin between the two men who each grabbed it at the same time.

"Mine!" each man screamed. Neither one would let go. "Mine!" They beat each other silly.

"Mine!" They beat each other bloody.

"Mine!" They beat and beat and beat each other dead.

"I will turn their greed and lust toward money," Satan continued explaining his plan. "They will forget about love; they will forget about life; they will forget about fairness; they will forget about giving; they will forget about family. You will not be able to restrain them, and by the time You become a grown man, they won't give two cents even to listen to You."

God hung His head.

"Oh — I can see that bothers You. You can get smaller and cover that one woman Mary. Or You can cover and protect the earth. But You can't have it both ways. Go ahead, though. Get smaller with that woman, but, in the meantime, they're going to be killing each other out here."

Satan left laughing; left God weeping. Dare He get any smaller and cover just one woman—and leave the world unprotected? Thousands would die, millions mistreated by those strong money-grippers.

Satan flew back to see how God was doing—but God was not there.

"He's not here. Not here? How can God be 'not here' if He is everywhere—unless—unless... No! He did it? I can't believe He chose the woman! Oh, for the hate of Pete, what can I do now? There He is, down there over that woman."

And then it struck Satan. He was now bigger than God.

"Oh, this is my big day. Now it's a simple matter from here on out. He cannot get inside her without getting smaller, but He cannot get any smaller and still cover her. The minute, the instant, he shrinks-even a smidgen—I'll shut tight every way into that woman. Then He'll be locked out with no way in, no way to get big again, and I will win."

So there God was, just about the size large enough to cover this one young woman. He dared not move—to the right or to the left. He had to think.

"I've got to get smaller to get inside of her. Once inside, I can get as small as necessary to start becoming a human being. But in order to get smaller, I've got to give up the last thing that makes Me big—My knowledge. I must let go of My mind."

The thought of letting go of His mind bothered Him considerably, because it meant He had only one chance to get inside of Mary. If it didn't work— He'd be small, no power, no reach, no mind to think of a new plan. It would simply be "finished."

Satan was watching God like a cat stalks a bird—ready to pounce. And ready he was. He had every move figured. The instant there was a sign of shrinking, he would lock up everything. He'd lock up her eyes. He'd lock up her ears. He'd lock up her mind, so God couldn't get in. Satan had become very good at helping people lock God out of their hearing, sight and thoughts. So he was sure he would be quicker than God, and every entrance would be shut and barred tight.

"Move—just one little move Little Fellow, and it will be Your last," his thin voice squeezed through cold, dripping lips.

God clung to the woman. His plan hadn't changed. He anticipated everything being locked up tight. It all depended on one thing—Mary's heart. He knew her heart. That's why He chose her. He felt sure it would remain open—and Satan could not touch it. But the entrance to it was so small—the chance so slim. He would have to let go of everything about Himself except one thing that can fit anywhere no matter how small.

He was ready. So the God of all knowledge bid one last farewell to His mind, whispered to Mary, *Here I come*, looked up at Satan, ready to pounce with locks and chains and bolts in his greasy hands, and said, **"Let there be no mind!"**

Now what took place next actually happened quicker than it takes you to forget to clean up your room. God started to shrink, and Satan saw it begin. First, He lost His knowledge of all the stars and planets. Satan sprang into action. Next, He lost His memory of how He created the world and all the animals. Satan rushed to Mary's eyes. Slam! Clank! Locked up tight!

"Ha-ha!" he howled. Next, God forgot how to add and subtract everything above five. Satan sprang to Mary's eyes. Crash! Clink! Locked up tight!

"He-he!" he teased.

Next, God lost His memory of every joke and riddle He ever thought up. He forgot when to say *Please* and *Thank you*. Smaller and smaller He got— so quick. He couldn't remember where He left His watch, the one that keeps track of when winter and summer begins. But the second He remembered He forgot His watch, He forgot what winter and summer were anyway. That bothered Him terribly, but just momentarily, because quickly He forgot what He had forgotten.

God's mind was shrinking with every "Ha-ha!" of Satan, who now was outside of Mary's mind— drilling holes and slipping in the bolts and twisting down the nuts.

"Ha-ha!" he howled

God lost His feeling.

"He-he!" he teased.

God lost His sight, His hearing. Everything His mind could do was almost gone. Last to go would be His voice. Satan twisted down the last nut.

God gathered up all that was left of Him, and in

the last second, just as His voice was about to turn to jibberjabber, He placed all of Himself right over the top of Mary's heart and screamed, **"Mary, I love y-o-o-ou!"**

And then He was gone.

Satan waited completely still... listening... looking... waiting. No God to be found. He went back and doublechecked every bolt and lock. All tight. Still he waited—and then he could contain himself no longer.

"Ha-ha!" he howled.

"He-he!" he teased.

Satan rolled with laughter. What delight! What crazy, insane, unexpected delight! God had shrunk Himself to nothing—nothing!

"Ha-ha!" he howled.

"He-he!" he teased.

He laughed until he collapsed in a heap draped across Mary's sleeping body.

"Ha-ha's" and "He-he's" were still sputtering through the big-lipped smile on his greasy face, when all of a sudden he thought he heard some faint sound from inside of Mary.

"Ho-ho, Satan."

"What?" he jerked.

"Ho-ho, Satan."

"Who is that?"

"Ho-ho, Satan."

"Where are you? Who are you?"

"Ho-ho, Satan. Ho-ho-ho-ho!"

Still confused—it seemed to Satan as if every "ha" and every "he" he had laughed was being swallowed one at a time by every "ho" he heard. And then he felt the kick. Something inside Mary kicked him!

"No-no!" he screamed. "No!"

"Ho-ho, Satan!"

"No! He got inside! No! No! No!"

And Satan ran off screaming into the far corner of the universe.

Now remember, all this happened in a kind of time we don't have here on earth. It doesn't go faster or slower. So by the time the *ha-ha's* were silent and the *ho-ho's* begun, Mary was just about ready to have the baby Jesus. And Jesus was being born at the very moment Satan was whimpering in the far corner of the universe.

Still, Satan was not so far away but what he couldn't see on the face of the ugly baby Jesus—that awful smile. It was a smile he'd seen before.

⁂

Well, that's my story for this year: what God had to go through to get small enough to get inside of Mary to become Jesus. By the time He was small enough, all that was left of Him was His love. But you might be interested to know how I found out about this amazing journey.

About 500 years ago, God called me into His Royal Chamber and said, "Enoch, I don't think people appreciate just how difficult it was for Me to get Myself—Someone so big—inside of Mary to become Jesus. So, as a reminder, I want you to go to earth and look up this fellow, Nicholas—or Santa, as I like to call him—the one I instructed to bring gifts every year to people all over the earth. Up until now, he has been leaving the gifts at people's front doors. Instead, tell him to do it by actually entering every single home. Now, of course, the doors will be locked and the windows latched tight.

So he will have to squeeze his big body and gifts down through the only way inside their warm homes—the narrow chimney flue. It will become part of the tradition.

"Let this tradition serve, for those who take notice, as a reminder of Me and what I went through to come to earth as Jesus."

His instruction being given, I turned to walk out the door. But just as I was about to pull the door shut, God called, "Enoch?"

I stuck my head back in, "Yes, Lord."

"When you see this Nicholas fellow…"

"Yes, Lord?"

"Tell him, when he visits people's houses…"

"Yes, Lord?"

"Tell him not to talk very much at all."

"Yes, Lord."

"In fact, Enoch, tell him just to say… 'Ho-ho.'"

Then God smiled. And from somewhere way off in the distance, I heard a faint scream.

"Yes, Lord," I nodded, "and a very, merry Ho-Ho indeed."

Why Stockings
Are Hung
At Christmastime

Remember me? My name is Enoch—the one heart-still-pumping human being in heaven. The one who every year brings you another story—a glimpse into what has been going on in heaven that is of interest to mortals like you and me around Christmastime.

For the past several years, I've been coming to you with stories involving the first Christmas when Jesus was born.

This year, you need to know that heaven didn't shut down after the first Christmas. God still has a lot of work going on every Christmas during the past 1989 years.

Recently my assignment has been to come and tell you these stories, but before this assignment, I've been involved in some special events all over the world.

And one year, my assignment involved Anthony Blodgett and his family. Now listen carefully.

Anthony Blodgett was nine and a half years old when he died. His mother was thirty-two. His father was often gone away. And his twin sisters, Kate and Sarah, were only four years old—and always in the way. At least they used to be, but now they weren't ever going to be in Anthony's way again, because he wasn't there anymore.

As I said, he was nine and a half when he died. I'm sorry to have to start this story off on such a sad note. But facts are facts. And death is death. And Anthony Blodgett was nine and a half years old when he died.

The year was 1795. The town was Massey's Cove, Connecticut. It was Christmas Eve. And the Blodgett house was especially cold.

Anthony's father, Benjamin Blodgett, bumped through the door with an armload of firewood. The fire in the living room fireplace of their two-story wood frame house had nearly gone out. Frost was squeezing through cracks around the windows, fighting to take possession of the Blodgett home.

It had been two weeks to the day since Anthony died.

Elizabeth, Anthony's Mom, was sitting at the kitchen window. A draft of bitter cold air stormed through the open door and penetrated her motionless thought.

"Benjamin," it was all she could do to speak, "what shall I do with these?" Laid across her lap were two nearly-completed wool socks. Actually, they were bigger than socks you are used to. They were called leggings, because they came all the way up children's legs.

"I don't know. They're too big for the twins. Too small for me."

"Just right for..." Elizabeth couldn't get out Anthony's name before tears stole away her shallow voice.

It was just the worst time of the year to lose a

child to pneumonia. There's never a good time, of course. But two weeks before Christmas... It's so cold. You have to stay inside so much—and see his things. Everywhere, his things—his schoolbooks, his clothes.

"...and these leggings. What am I going to do with these leggings?" Elizabeth let them drop to the floor.

Kate and Sarah heard their Daddy come in. *Maybe he had brought Anthony with him.* They hurried into the living room to see. They still didn't understand what it meant for someone to be dead. Whenever Daddy was gone for two weeks trading furs in Vermont, Daddy came home. They couldn't understand where Anthony went, but they did expect him to come back. Around the corner they ran, slipping on the bare wood floor, "Daddy! Daddy! Did Anthony come with you?"

Benjamin looked helplessly toward his wife, then down at the floor, "No." He laid down the armload of wood near the fireplace, picked up the poker, and began to stir the ashes, looking for one or two live coals to glow red. Something to get the fire burning again. Something to get... something...

He remembered two weeks ago at Anthony's bedside, praying, hoping for *one or two breaths, a beat of the heart — something to get him living again. Please... Nothing.*

It was 1795 in Massey's Cove, Connecticut, Christmas Eve — and here was an empty family. Not everyone wants Christmas to come. Not everyone is happy at Christmastime. My assignment was the Blodgett family.

I knocked on the door. Sarah and Kate opened it.

"Kewee, mee eyes must be seein' double, er me 'ead went daff. I could swear on me Uncle Dudley's gold teeth that 'ere ye 'ave two o' the prettiest young lassies me eyes 'ave ever 'ad the pleasure of settin' upon, in all me live long years!"

You'll have to forgive me. I should explain. One of the benefits of heaven is language. All sorts of languages. We have them all up there — tongues of men and angels.

My favorite is Cockney. I love calling the Lord, "Guvnor." He sometimes plays along if He doesn't have other things pressing and calls me, "Mate."

Anyways—God sent me to the Blodgetts to see if I could find a way to give them comfort and a special note at Christmastime. A perfect opportunity for me to have a fling at my Cockney accent—seeing how I had to assume the disguise of a traveller needing lodging.

"Who is it, Kate?" asked Benjamin, still tending the fire. "Just some stranger, Daddy!"

"Well, let him in and close the door."

I shook off the snow, stamped my feet and stepped into the house.

"'ullo," I said. "It's a bit o' not alright out there. Sure do appreciate the invite inta yer 'ouse. Wouldn't 'ave a lit'l spot o' tea to warm me frozen bones?"

Elizabeth stood up and walked over to the cupboard.

"Where are you coming from?" she asked as she reached for the tea in the cupboard.

"Come again, Mum?"

"I said, where are you coming from?" Her voice strained for enough energy to get the words through the cold air.

"Me? I've been way up north fer quite a few years, Mum. Decided to come down 'ere fer a spell."

Benjamin sensed his wife's struggle to converse, and stepped in, "Where you headed tonight?"

"Me? Tonight? Well—er—I'd sorta 'oped this would be me stoppin' place. Seems 'ow it's dark and bitter cold out there. Isn't much better in 'ere. You folks got rabbit fur underwear?"

Sarah and Kate giggled.

"You mean I was right? You do 'ave rabbit fur underwear."

"No, we do not," they said in unison, looked at each other and giggled again.

"Then 'ows come you let the 'ouse keep so cold? Now won't you tell me that?"

The answer was immediate. "Because our brother, Anthony, has gone away..." said Kate. "And Daddy and Mama spend lots of time talking."

"Yeah, and the fire goes out before Daddy notices," added Sarah, to conclude the explanation.

I looked at Elizabeth, who handed me a cup of tea and looked away quickly.

"Gone away now 'as 'e?" I said to the girls, as I straightened up to face Benjamin, "and I don't s'pose 'e's comin' back, is 'e, Mate?"

"No—pneumonia."

"I'm sorry—now I am—real sorry, fer troublin' ye at such a time as this. I'll just finish me tea an' be on me way."

At that, Elizabeth spun around. "You'll do no such thing—you'll spend the night here with us."

She didn't seem very overjoyed to make the offer. But she did what she did because that's what people did in those days.

By now, Benjamin had the fire going good and strong. Kate and Sarah got as close to it as possible without their toes catching fire. Soon they had fallen asleep on the floor while we grown-ups talked.

"So tell me, Mum, tell me about it..."

For the next hour, Elizabeth struggled to discuss Anthony's struggle for life. When she spoke about his labored breathing—she herself fought for air. She pressed her right palm against her upper chest as she tried to imitate the rattling sound in his lungs. Then she slumped into Benjamin's arms—staring silently.

It was agony for her—reliving Anthony's last week of life. Actually, it was worse than the week itself. At least then when he cried, she could hold him, rub his chest, sing a quiet song—be a mother. Now she had these memories—so real, but no Anthony. Nothing she could do in response to the sights and sounds her mind reviewed.

"I can't bear the thought. I'm only thirty-two. Twenty-five or thirty more years without him."

"Ay, Mum—but can ye imagine the past nine and a half years without 'im? Would ye rather not 'ave 'ad 'im at all?"

"But why would God give him to us, then take him away like that?"

❦❧

Now that was an interesting question. It had been a couple thousand years since I had thought that one. I remember when I was alive on earth, I told myself—*I'm going to ask God one day why He lets children die.*

But when I finally did go to heaven, I never even thought to ask it. In fact, it wasn't until I heard it from Elizabeth's lips that I remembered *that was a question I wanted an answer for.*

Why hadn't I ever remembered to ask that question? Well, to this day, I'm not certain. And even when I went back to heaven after visiting the Blodgetts, I intended to ask God, but forgot all about it again.

It's a good question—why He lets children die—and deserves an answer. I keep forgetting until I'm back down here. The best I can figure is this: When I'm on earth, away from God, I'm faced with all sorts of good questions. But when I'm in heaven, I'm faced with a *good* God. When you're actually right there with Him, you're so sure that everything about Him is good and perfect. And when you're sure that every answer will be good, it just doesn't seem to be as important to ask the question. And I forget… until I'm back here.

❦ ❧

So I had no answer for Elizabeth. "That's a good question, Mum. I've been waitin' a number a years to ask that'un meself. You'll 'ave to try askin' God yerself."

"Oh, I plan to—I plan to."

"Good luck, Mum. But I'll be surprised if ye remember." I almost let too much slip out. Elizabeth looked at me hard and long for the first time—in wonderment—concerning my identity.

"Who are you, Sir?" she asked.

"Me? Mum? Me name's Enoch, Mum."

Before she asked "Enoch, who?"—I wouldn't have had an answer for that because I didn't have a last name then and still don't—Benjamin stood up, went over to the fire, leaned across the sleeping twins to toss a couple more logs on the fire that was starting to get lazy and dim.

"I'll carry the girls into bed," he offered.

While Benjamin did that, Elizabeth went into the kitchen, picked up the wool leggings she had dropped on the floor earlier, brought them to me, and laid them across my lap with the question, "Tell me, what shall I do with these now? They were for Anthony, for Christmas."

That's when the idea came to me, and I knew what God wanted me to do for the Blodgetts.

"I'd say, finish 'em, Mum. Finish 'em."

"Finish them? Whatever for?"

"Fer Anthony, Mum. As long as 'e don't 'ave

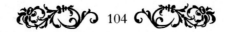 104

need uv 'em, I'm sure 'e'd love to 'ave you wearin' um. They'd be just yer size, Mum. Just yer size—indeed."

That was a brand new thought for Elizabeth. *Finish the leggings.* I could tell the idea was fighting for possession of her heart, but there was a struggle going on inside. Those unfinished leggings presented her with the biggest decision she had ever faced.

I said goodnight and asked Benjamin to show me to my bed for the night.

"Goodnight, Mum. Pleasant dreams."

Elizabeth just sat there, lost in a battle over yarn and needles.

I went into the bedroom and shut the door around, nearly closed, but left open ever so slightly. I set the note God had given me addressed to Elizabeth on the night stand and kicked my legs up into bed. I didn't undress. I didn't plan to stay until daybreak.

❧⟊⟊⟊❧

Most of that night, a soft, flickering light from the living room slid sideways through my unshut door. I listened. Benjamin and Elizabeth never spoke. He tended the fire. I heard only the sound of the rocking chair, the crackling of the fire, and the gentle melody of Elizabeth's voice singing to Anthony as she knitted her way out of sorrow into a future without her son. Every knit and purl came at a great price.

After several hours, the light went out. Only the dim glow of the fire lit the home as I slipped out of my bedroom into the living room. There, hanging from the mantel over the fireplace, was Anthony's leggings, bright red with a small white band at the top. I didn't understand what they were doing so close to the fire, until I went over to read the note sticking up out of one legging and felt they were wet from her tears. The note simply read:

> *To Anthony,*
> *I finished them for you.*
> *Love,*
> *Mother*

I took that note and put in its place the message God gave me, turned and walked out of the Blodgett home into the near-dawn darkness.

Later the next morning, Elizabeth awoke to squeals. "The man's gone, Mama! The man's gone!"

Elizabeth threw on her robe and looked in the room I had vacated. When she saw I wasn't there, she went into the living room to stoke the fire.

That's when she saw the words — To Elizabeth — sticking up out of the now-dry leggings.

Puzzled and curious, she hesitated, then slowly pulled the note from the stocking and began to read:

> *To Elizabeth,*
> *Anthony knows.*
> *Merry Christmas.*

The year was 1795. The town was Massey's Cove, Connecticut. The day was Christmas. And the Blodgett home was especially warm.

Well, that's my story for this year. But now I suppose you guessed that every year after that, Elizabeth Blodgett asked Kate and Sarah to hang their stockings on the mantel so she could take what was empty and fill them with gifts of love. Just like God had done for her.

Printed in the United States
29304LVS00007B/469-519